I0628006

Demented

Atlantic City's Most Wanted #2

Charity Parkerson

Punk & Sissy Publications

Copyright

—Warning: This book is intended for readers over the age of 18. Some of my books contain allusions to past abuse and trauma.

CONTENTS

Introduction

*There's nothing Lazarus loves **more** than a mystery. Noir has him stumped. That's how people like him get killed.*

On paper, Lazarus doesn't exist. He's a ghost. An assassin. He's also likely the worst thing to ever happen to Noir. Noir is part of the elite. Lazarus came from trash and will probably die there. They shouldn't have met. In fact, their meeting is a bit too convenient.

Noir is a lot of things. Bored, rich, and part of the upper crust. He's also a prince and the biggest drug kingpin on the east coast. No one has ever gotten close enough to him to know that part. Unfortunately, that makes him the guy Lazarus is hunting to kill. It's a predicament to be sure, especially since neither of them has ever wanted anyone else as badly.

Demented is the second book in Charity Parkerson's Atlantic City's Most Wanted series. These are sexy and sometimes dark stories where the richest and most dangerous men in Atlantic City meet their match. These are best enjoyed when read in order.

AUTHOR NOTE

THIS IS A DARK romance series, including murder, abuse, drug use, and crime lords. If you haven't read the prequel, Captivated, you might want to start there. Thanks for reading!

CHAPTER ONE

EIGHT MONTHS. THAT WAS how long Lazarus had his knees in the dirt. He had followed people, spent countless hours watching houses, and rubbed elbows with trash. Of course, most people would argue he was trash. It was likely true. More than the countless tattoos and scars, Lazarus also gave off a vibe. He knew it. It was impossible to escape. He was a twisted psychopath. Lazarus had never sweated that. He got paid extremely well to embrace his insanity. Lazarus killed people for a living. He very desperately wanted to find the head of the snake and dissect it, sending pieces of it to everyone they hurt. Whoever ran the drug trade in Atlantic City was more protected than anyone Lazarus had ever seen, but Lazarus was close. He felt it.

Unfortunately, whereas Lazarus blended well with the dregs of society, power always spewed upward. The closer Lazarus got, the more he stood out. That was fine. He still had his ways. Everyone liked to gamble. Atlantic City Casinos were the perfect spot to cross paths with the elite. It was nothing for them to sit at a table and lose money all day. Fortunately, poor people did that too.

Lazarus pushed the button on the slot machine where he sat every couple of minutes to keep up pretenses. Meanwhile, his gaze never stopped moving toward the closest poker table. More specifically to Andreas Bouras. Andreas was a high roller. He obviously came from money, and he was every bit as deadly as Lazarus. The only difference between them was who pulled the strings.

Eight months ago, someone had ordered a hit on Lazarus' friend's husband. Lazarus had itched to kill the bastard who attacked Gable. In his sleep. Like a coward. When they found his attacker dead, Lazarus might have let it go, except the guy's death pecked at the back of Lazarus' brain. They found him stabbed to death with a note pinned to his chest, stating they were square. Lazarus' obsession started with the mystery of it all. The more this guy eluded him, the more Lazarus needed to bathe in his blood. No one escaped him. He had a reputation to uphold.

Months of work had led him here: Andreas. Lazarus sat feet from the man who knew the answers to Lazarus' questions. He couldn't take the guy here. Casinos were mob territory. Even Lazarus wasn't that stupid. Casinos were neutral ground. Lazarus might get his hands on Andreas, but it would be the last thing he did. He didn't want that. It wasn't good enough to squeeze Andreas. Lazarus needed the name of his boss. That was all. He was prepared to cut that name from his tongue.

"Does he owe you money?"

Lazarus' head whipped around at the question. A man with perfectly styled brown hair and dead-looking light green eyes sat with a drink in one hand, looking comfortable yet bored. It was obvious he had been sitting there for a minute. No one ever sneaked up on him. Yet this guy had. "I don't know what you mean."

The man dipped his chin toward Andreas. "You've been watching him like he owes you money." The guy paused. "Or fucked your dog, for a good hour, and that's only as long as I've been here. I have no idea how long before that."

Lazarus fell back on being personable. He was a firm believer in fetching more flies with honey than vinegar. Until the moment he slit someone's throat, anyhow. "Do you know firsthand how someone looks at a person who's fucked their dog?"

A sexy chuckle fell from the man's lips.

A hunger hit Lazarus he hadn't experienced in a while: white-hot desire. Lazarus didn't want people. If he got the itch, he simply screwed the first willing person. He didn't even care about their gender. It was rare as hell for anyone to actually pull an emotion from him.

"A sense of humor. That always makes a man twice as sexy."

Lazarus' eyebrows rose. The guy was average size and build. He was polished—like he had never seen the inside of a public school. There was a definite slight accent filled with the boredom of the elite. He obviously came from wealth, which meant he was lazy and by no means ready to get wiped across the floor by someone Lazarus' size. Yet he had made a comment like that to Lazarus with no clue of Lazarus' sexual orientation. Lazarus' lust doubled. Bravery mixed with confidence was sexy as fuck.

"I'm Lazarus."

"Does I'm Lazarus have a last name?"

Nothing about him was real, so it didn't matter. "Melnyk."

The guy leaned forward, holding Lazarus' stare. "Noir Antonsen."

Danish. Yum. He recognized the accent now. It wasn't heavy. Just enough to make him interesting. "Nice to meet you."

"You, as well." Noir stood, and Lazarus learned why he hadn't been afraid to flirt with him. Several men in black suits with earpieces appeared like wraiths. "Perhaps we'll meet again sometime."

It wasn't often Lazarus was stunned. Equally, no one ever got the drop on him. He hadn't spotted a single security guard, especially an entire team. Lazarus tried not to show his shock. "I'd like that."

Noir smirked. It was hot.

"The car has been brought around, Your Highness."

Lazarus was floored. He worried he might have to pick his jaw up from the floor.

Noir barely spared the man a glance. "Good." He focused on Lazarus. "Are you coming?"

Goddamn. A man used to getting everything he wanted. The temptation was thick. "Sorry. I've got business."

"That's too bad." Noir turned away. He was quickly swallowed by security on his way out.

Lazarus watched until he couldn't see him any longer. He really wanted to kick himself for declining the invitation. Lazarus knew a bad decision when he saw one. Noir was definitely that. His gaze moved back toward the poker table. Fucking hell. Andreas was gone. With a growl, Lazarus dug out his phone. There was no sense in scouring the casino for him. The place was huge and Lazarus didn't know how long he had been gone. He should have left with Noir. Lazarus opened his web browser and searched for Noir's name. His shoulders fell at the immediate flood of results. That security guy hadn't been playing. *His Royal Highness,*

Noir Antonsen. Prince of The Republic of Serveno. So, not Danish. A smaller county nearby, though. Lazarus had been close. Goddamn it. Lazarus would never get within five feet of the guy again. Fucking royalty. Nothing like ruining his own shot, all to follow a guy who had vanished. For fuck's sake. What a day.

The moment Noir climbed into the back of his SUV, he opened his messages. He knew the report would be waiting. His people were the best in the world. Lazarus Melnyk had Noir's alarm bells clanging. There was no reason for him to be following Andreas. No good reason, anyhow. The file was waiting, as expected. Unexpectedly, it was nearly empty. Lazarus Melnyk. No middle name. Forty-two. That was it. People didn't have nothing in this day and age. Everyone had a digital footprint of some kind. The only people who had nothing were trouble.

"What do you want us to do?"

Noir eyed his personal guard. Ajax had been with him since Noir was a child. Not once had he treated Noir like he had watched him grow up. Noir was his prince. Always would be. "Put a tail on him and send Andreas on a trip. I think he needs a tropical vacation somewhere off the map."

Ajax nodded. "I'm on it." He pulled out his phone and started typing.

Noir stared out the window. He had been rejected. Noir wanted to laugh. Lazarus was nearly twice his age. He definitely looked as if he had seen some things. Not once had Noir been accused of slumming it. Lazarus was definitely not his usual style. The hard body, scars, and tattoos. The facial hair with just a touch of gray. Damn. He was intrigued. Lazarus looked intelligent. He had to be to have gotten this close to Noir. Of course, he didn't know it.

The phone in his hand rang. Noir didn't recognize the number, but not just anyone could call him. He answered. "Yes?"

"I think I was a little hasty turning down your offer."

Noir froze. His gaze slid to Ajax. "How did you get this number?"

Ajax immediately went on alert.

A sexy laugh rumbled through the phone. "I'm very resourceful."

Noir hummed. "Perhaps you can tell me about these resources over dinner? You choose the place."

Another delicious laugh caressed Noir's ear. "Where does one take an entire security team for dinner?"

A smile snapped to Noir's face. "In my experience, any damn where I want. Don't worry. You won't even know they're there."

Ajax stared at Noir with a puzzled look.

Noir ignored him. "So what do you say? Do you plan to turn me down again?"

There was a pause.

Noir held his breath. He was more intrigued than he cared to admit.

"There's a restaurant called Alexander's on Ninth."

Noir curled his nose but didn't argue. He had never eaten there, but Noir was accustomed to more upscale places. "I've seen it."

"Meet me there at seven."

"I can do that."

"Good. I'll see you then."

Noir tried not to smile again. Ajax already looked suspicious. "See you." He disconnected the call. "I'm to meet him at Alexander's at seven."

Ajax dipped his chin. "I'll set up everything. Someone with no background is dangerous. I'd say this is a terrible idea, but this is the best way to determine his motives."

Noir nodded. "Agreed." He kept his tone bland and his thoughts to himself. There was no way he would admit to being interested in someone so beneath him. Then again, the guy didn't exist on paper. Maybe they weren't that different after all.

CHAPTER TWO

LAZARUS ARRIVED TEN MINUTES early, hoping to watch the door to see if he could track a pattern for Noir's security. Noir was already seated at a table, looking relaxed and unbothered by everything. He was stunning. People looked his way constantly. If Noir noticed, he gave no clues. Lazarus watched Noir take a drink of ice water from a wineglass. He winced. Lazarus chuckled under his breath. He had intentionally chosen a place where Noir would be out of place. Lazarus wanted him unbalanced.

As Lazarus headed his way, Noir's light green gaze landed on him. Hunger punched Lazarus. He had a driving need to shake up Noir's boring existence. Lazarus wanted to twist him. Sully him. He brought out the darkest of Lazarus' needs.

Lazarus slid into the booth across from him. "Is it odd I'm surprised you showed?"

A hint of humor touched Noir's features. "Do you get stood up a lot?"

Lazarus shrugged. "I don't date."

"Hmm. Doesn't date and has the resources to find me. Interesting."

Lazarus didn't want him too curious. Noir likely had the connections to find out anything he wanted about Lazarus. He didn't want Noir digging. "He didn't give me your number, but my best friend is Cutler Maine. That gives me some connections in your circle." There. Cutler wasn't his best friend.

It seemed they were friends, as far as people like them had friends. Honestly, they were more like colleagues. He didn't know what they were. Lazarus liked Cutler more than most, he supposed. Mostly, Lazarus just needed to douse Noir's curiosity.

"Ah." Noir nodded. "An assassin. That explains a lot."

Lazarus froze.

Noir smirked. "You're not the only one who knows things. I'm observant."

Lazarus couldn't believe his ears. "You're observant." He didn't know why he repeated Noir's claim. There was just no way he had observed that.

A sexy chuckle rumbled from Noir.

Lazarus cleared his throat. He wiped his palms on his thighs. "That doesn't bother you?" Food and a beer appeared in front of him. Lazarus blinked.

"I ordered for us. The less time we have to sit here, the better."

It seemed as if Lazarus should have some complaint, but everything Noir chose was perfect. "Uh. Thanks."

Noir waited until the server moved away to get back to their earlier topic. "Why would I be bothered?" It took Lazarus a second to recall where their conversation had left off. Noir didn't wait for him to answer. "I have no reason to concern myself with anyone else's business. To be honest, I don't care enough."

Fuck. That was oddly hot. He was the picture of an unconcerned, bored, and spoiled elitist. Yet something about him reminded Lazarus of himself. He had never fucked anyone who knew his secrets. Lazarus didn't have to guard his every thought and word.

He couldn't decide how he felt. Noir likely couldn't prove his observation, but he could force Lazarus to run if he talked. Lazarus had intended to unbalance Noir. Instead, he was the one thrown off his game.

"I see," Noir said when Lazarus still hadn't found his voice. "You think I'm just an empty-headed royal?"

That spurred Lazarus' brain into action. "No. I think you're too intelligent for your own good." Lazarus paused, trying to decide if he would continue. His mouth chose for him. "And incredibly sexy. I don't think I've ever been this turned on by anyone."

Noir's mouth lifted in one corner. "We'll see." He took a bite of his food, leaving Lazarus still reeling from only a short fifteen-minute conversation. Lazarus was more than aroused and intrigued. He was downright obsessed with the need to know more. Lazarus had never been this focused on a target he didn't intend to kill. Noir was fascinating as hell. Lazarus was hooked.

Dinner was enlightening. If—at any time—people wanted to understand other people, all it always took was one look at their friends. He knew Lazarus hadn't expected admitting a friendship with Cutler would expose him. Perhaps it wouldn't have if they weren't so different. Cutler was part of the upper crust. Atlantic City crème de la crème. The only way someone like Lazarus would be on the same level as Cutler was to know him by trade. Still, it had been a slight risk by saying the words aloud. Of course, he could have played the accusation off as a joke if he had been wrong.

But the moment Lazarus had named Cutler, the clouds had cleared. Everything about Lazarus made sense. Noir would be amazed if Lazarus was even the guy's name. Unfortunately, the revelation also explained Lazarus' earlier laser focus on Andreas. If someone had a contract on Noir's top supplier, Noir needed to know who and why. Not quite as unfortunately, that meant Noir wasn't finished with Lazarus yet. He could have Ajax torture the information from him, but why? Noir wasn't bored yet.

Outside the restaurant, they stood next to a Harley that obviously belonged to Lazarus. Noir honestly didn't want the night to end. "I'd invite you back to my place, but you've already shot me down once today."

Lazarus flipped open the saddlebag on his bike and produced a second helmet. "How about a counteroffer? Come with me?" He acted as if he planned to hand the helmet to

Noir before pulling it back again. "Of course, your security team won't fit on my bike."

Noir fought a smile. This guy. He was something else. "I adore that you obviously think they can't stay on your tail and invisible. Do you have any idea what it takes to be a royal guard? Even your SEALs could never."

"It probably takes at least a quarter of your arrogance, so I'm sure they're talented."

A bark of laughter burst from Noir without his permission. Noir never laughed. Life had stopped entertaining him years ago. "More than a quarter." He accepted the helmet and made a quick gesture, alerting his team to follow. Nearby headlights fired to life. "It's only fair to warn you, though. If you kill me on this thing, you'll likely be beheaded."

Lazarus' smile never wavered. "Fair enough."

After donning the helmet, he climbed on behind Lazarus. His hands slid across the man's stomach as he scooted in close to hang on. Soft flesh over solid muscle stirred a dark hunger inside him. This man was a killer. A hunter. A predator. And Noir was demented. He craved the violence. Noir wanted to get fucked. The longer he stayed pressed against Lazarus' back, the larger his hunger grew. Lazarus drove along the coast. Noir's hands found their way beneath Lazarus' shirt before moving lower. He knew he played a dangerous game. His teasing could get them killed, but Lazarus seemed to have ironclad self-control. That detail only made Noir hotter. Lazarus would be focused. Noir wanted that.

Lazarus suddenly veered onto an almost invisible beach-way entry. Noir didn't question anything. His mind was too far gone. At the end of the road, there was a small beach house. It was hidden from sight—like it had been built specifically to be advertised as a secluded honeymoon getaway. Before Noir had time to think, he was over Lazarus' shoulder and headed through the door. The place was dark inside. His helmet went flying before his back hit the inside of the closed front door.

"Fucking tease." Lazarus' mouth covered his. His hands were everywhere. Noir was so aroused, he couldn't breathe. Lazarus tore at his clothes, stripping him so deftly Noir barely noticed. Noir let it happen. This was what he wanted—to feel alive. He needed someone desperate for him. Noir didn't want to think anymore.

Noir pushed Lazarus' shirt up until Lazarus took the hint and let him have it. He only got the quick glance before Lazarus was on him again, but wow. Noir's hunger doubled. He was perfect, and all that ink... yum.

While in a lust-filled haze, Noir watched Lazarus tear into foil packages, using his teeth. He didn't even know where they came from. Then his mouth was back. He controlled Noir, fingering him with wet fingers. When his feet left the floor, Noir scrambled to keep up. His legs wrapped around Lazarus' hips like they belonged there. Lazarus shoved his arm between his body and Noir's leg, manipulating Noir's body into the position he wanted. He did it so easily—like Noir weighed nothing. Noir had never been more invested. Lazarus dictated every move. Noir was just along for the ride. Then Lazarus impaled him. Noir made a sound he had never even heard before. It was pleasure and surrender.

Lazarus held his stare as he lifted and lowered Noir, using his body like a toy. He openly studied Noir's every reaction. There was no emotion in his expression. He was a cold perfectionist, taking what he wanted while ensuring Noir enjoyed every second. If Noir wasn't so crazed with need, he might have been turned off by the disconnect. But Lazarus was a magician. His every move was meant to please. Noir almost felt like some sort of science project, and he was prepared to beg for every second of it.

Then Lazarus' lips parted on a pant. He suddenly didn't look as in control. Noir couldn't look away. Sweat coated Lazarus' torso. He leaned into things. Noir's vision swam. Everything felt amazing. His body was twisted with the need to reach the edge. He held his breath as his muscles tensed.

"Give it to me."

Until that moment, Noir hadn't even noticed the silence. But the sound of Lazarus' hungry demand sent Noir flying. His entire body twitched as he cried out, unable to control the sounds he made. His vision dimmed as his body jerked and shook. Cum flew through the space between them. A drop hit Lazarus' lip. Noir had never come so hard in his life. Lazarus' tongue shot out, licking away the cum. Noir swore he couldn't even blink. He was immersed. Lazarus' breath hitched. His eyes fell closed. That was it. He didn't make a sound. The muscle in his jaw worked overtime—like he bit back all the sounds as he fought to stay silent. It was fascinating. Noir couldn't look away. He memorized every detail. When Lazarus' eyes opened and he focused on Noir again, Noir's heart stopped as the full ramifications hit. This guy was a monster. He wouldn't stop until he found his prey. Noir was totally fucked.

Lazarus was fully aware Noir played a game far out of his league. Since he didn't own a conscience, Lazarus couldn't care. He had gotten what he wanted. Noir hadn't made Lazarus work for it at all—other than the amazing workout. But to be real, he needed that. He had been too focused on Andreas. His routine had fallen a bit to the wayside.

Oddly, Noir sat on the couch and toyed with his phone, looking unmoved by their encounter. That bugged Lazarus, and he didn't know why. Maybe he was off his game or something. Lazarus definitely shouldn't care. They had both gotten off. Noir's feelings shouldn't matter. He shouldn't matter.

Noir stood and shoved his phone in his back pocket. "My guards are waiting. If I don't resurface soon, they might storm the place."

Lazarus blinked. "Okay." He didn't know what else to say. It wasn't like he wanted to cuddle or some shit, but he also hadn't expected Noir to leave immediately.

"Thank you for dinner."

Lazarus literally had nothing. "Okay."

Noir headed for the door.

Without thinking, Lazarus stepped into his path. He didn't have a plan. Lazarus simply covered Noir's mouth with his. He had no clue why. This kiss wouldn't lead to sex. So why had he done this? He pulled away and spent a moment staring at Noir up close. Noir was incredibly beautiful with his gorgeous green eyes and the smattering of light freckles Lazarus hadn't noticed earlier. Something funny happened to Lazarus' chest. He looked young—much younger than Lazarus had realized. Lazarus hadn't taken the time to truly dig into Noir's life. He had gotten carried away at the idea of touching someone so far out of his reach. It was ridiculous, but he had been born poor white trash and no amount of money had changed that knowledge. He tattooed his skin and fit in places this boy never would. For a wild moment, Lazarus had wanted to taste what he could never have or be. Too late, he saw Noir as a person.

"I had a good time."

One side of Noir's mouth lifted in a wry smile—like he knew Lazarus' every word was bullshit, and he would never hear from Lazarus again. "See you around." Noir stepped around him and let himself out.

Lazarus stood in the middle of the living room like a statue. He had no idea how long he stood there before reality returned.

Lazarus found his phone and searched Noir's name again. This time, he paid attention to every detail. His birthdate. Where he stood in line of succession. What his titles and responsibilities were. It was all fascinating, but that birthdate held his focus much longer than he liked. It didn't take much math to figure out Noir was only twenty-four. Fuck. Lazarus didn't even recall being that young. This entire night had been a mistake. It wasn't guilt he felt exactly. Lazarus didn't do guilt. This was something else. He couldn't put a name to the emotion since he didn't have many of those. Lazarus just felt off—wrong. He needed to get back to work and find Andreas again. Lazarus had to do whatever it took to get out of this town and back to his life on the road. Maybe uncovering this mystery wasn't worth staying in one spot this long. After all, the man who attacked Gable was dead. Surely that was enough.

Lazarus headed for the bedroom and grabbed his go-bag. He made it to the door before his feet froze. Something stirred in his gut. Lazarus didn't like it. His phone buzzed. Lazarus checked the device.

Noir: *I had a good time too.*

Without another thought, Lazarus dropped the bag. He couldn't walk away from this mystery. Not yet. A tiny voice in the back of his mind whispered, Lazarus knew the truth about why he was staying. It didn't matter. Lazarus never left a job undone. He wouldn't leave this one either. Unfortunately, Lazarus no longer knew if he meant Andreas or Noir.

CHAPTER THREE

MIMOSAS BY THE OCEAN. Noir inhaled the salty air. With his eyes closed, he let the breeze wash over him. He allowed himself a moment of peace. Noir didn't take his breakfast outside often, but it was a gorgeous day. He wanted to savor the sound of waves lapping. Everything looked brighter for some reason he couldn't name. At least, that was the lie he told himself.

"Lucas is here, Your Highness."

With a sigh, Noir opened his eyes. There was always something that needed his attention. "Send him out here."

The tall, skinny red-haired man who worked in Noir's circles stepped out onto the balcony. He looked nervous. It wasn't often he saw Noir. There was always a buffer between him and anyone who might try to take him down... like Lazarus.

Noir motioned to the chair across from him. "Please, sit." He moved a champagne glass Lucas' way. "Have a drink."

A servant rushed forward and poured a mimosa for Lucas. Lucas didn't touch it. "Thank you. Ajax said you need to speak to me."

Ah, jumping right in. Definitely nervous. Noir stood and put his hands in the pockets of his robe. He paced, circling behind Lucas as he spoke. "I heard a rumor you gave out my number."

Lucas didn't turn. He held himself rigid. "I did, but—at the time—I definitely didn't see a problem."

Noir pulled the knife from his pocket and moved to stand directly behind Lucas. "Why exactly did you think that I would be okay with you handing out my personal information?"

"Because it was Jericho Wrath."

That gave Noir pause. He slid the knife bank in his pocket. "Jericho?" Jericho ran a charity for child victims of sex trafficking. Even though the charity was real, it was secretly run by the Russian mafia.

Lucas finally turned and nodded. "He said his husband recently put together a charity event in our area and would be interested in possibly teaming up with you for another.

Someone on his staff gave him my number and so on and so forth."

Noir glanced toward Ajax. Ajax shrugged. He was obviously just as lost as Noir. Noir padded back to his seat. So, more than one person had given out his number? Was it a coincidence that Lazarus had gotten his number the same day as Lucas had given it to Jericho? Or was Jericho one of Lazarus' many connections? If so, fuck. Noir tried not to show his concern. "That would be good for the family's reputation."

Lucas nodded. "That's what I thought. Your dad said he wanted to see more positive things coming from this area. That's why I didn't even hesitate. If I was wrong, I apologize. Under any other circumstances, I never would've given anyone your number."

Noir settled deeper in his seat and took a sip of his drink. "I'm glad we were able to clear this up. It was quite a surprise for my phone to ring yesterday."

Lucas looked confused. "Yesterday? Huh. He said it would likely be a week or two before he called. His people wanted to have a solid plan for you before starting the discussion. That's why I hadn't told you. I knew I would see you later this week, and I thought I had time to give you a heads-up."

Every second that ticked by, Noir's confusion grew. On one hand, he had definitely benefited from Lazarus finding his number. On the other, he couldn't have his people exposing him. Then there was the whole question of whether this incident was even related to Lazarus finding him. Noir didn't know what to think.

"Hmm. Well." Noir couldn't let Lucas know it hadn't been Jericho who called. Just in case there was a leak somewhere, he didn't need that hole to get bigger. He might look weak. "You're here. You might as well enjoy breakfast with me. We can discuss business now and cancel our meeting for later this week."

Lucas smiled. His shoulders visibly relaxed. "That sounds good."

Noir didn't have to ask. Plates appeared on the table. Noir inhaled the scent of properly seasoned food. Whatever he had eaten the night before had sat on his stomach the entire night.

"Oh, good. I'm right on time."

Noir's head whipped toward the door. Lazarus strolled onto the balcony. Ajax looked at him for guidance. Noir motioned for him to stand down. They still had a witness. Noir couldn't show his home as having weak spots in its security. Lucas needed to think Lazarus had been invited.

"Good morning, Lazarus. I wasn't expecting you." He paused for effect. "Quite this early."

Lazarus wore a shit-eating grin. It was obvious he enjoyed getting the drop on Noir. "Well, you know, I was already in the neighborhood."

Noir tossed Lucas an apologetic smile. "It seems we'll be keeping our meeting after all."

The closest servant grabbed Lucas' plate. "I'll wrap this up for you to go."

Being a smart man, Lucas immediately stood. "I'll see you then." He headed inside, nodding at Lazarus as he passed.

Lazarus watched him go. "No 'Your Highness' this time?"

"Lucas isn't from my country. I'm not his prince."

Lazarus claimed the seat Lucas vacated. "Do you find it disrespectful when people don't bow to you here?"

A smirk pulled at Noir's lips. "Who says people don't bow to me here?" He immediately turned serious. "You seem to be finding all the gaps in my security. It's looking more and more like I need to hire you."

"Keeping people safe isn't in my skill set."

Fuck. Why did he find this guy so hot? They were equally fucked in the head. They had no business playing this game. "What brings you by this morning?"

Lazarus' gaze swept down his body. "You're actually wearing a robe. I swear this entire setup is like something from a movie. Do you actually live like this?"

He knew Lazarus wanted him to feel like some pretentious asshole. Noir had been raised in the height of luxury. He couldn't be bothered to care how that looked to anyone else. Noir was royalty. He would damn well live like a prince. "Do you actually live in a one-room hut on the beach while eating greasy food every night?"

Lazarus' eyebrows rose. "Damn. You really are a snob."

Noir made a dismissive motion. "You started it. I thought we were simply making observations."

Lazarus sat forward and tossed back Lucas' untouched drink. "Actually, I live in Arizona. Deep in the desert, to be precise. I'm only here on business."

Ah. Pride was his weakness. Noir knew now how to dig out his secrets. "The man you were stalking yesterday?"

"No. I want his boss."

Noir had suspected as much. Little did Lazarus know he sat across from him. "Does the boss owe you money?"

Lazarus' face hardened. "The boss ordered my friend's husband killed. He didn't succeed and he won't because I don't stop until I find my target."

Actually, Noir had not ordered his friend's death. That was exactly why the man responsible had paid with his life. Noir didn't deal with people who risked his business over their bruised pride. He was a professional. "Well, good luck, I suppose." He would need it. There was zero chance he could link anything to Noir.

A servant set food in front of Lazarus, pausing their conversation.

Lazarus waited until they were somewhat alone again before speaking. "Your level of unconcern still confuses me. Your guards should be tossing me out."

Noir plucked a strawberry from his plate. "Do I have reason to be worried?" He ate his berry while waiting for Lazarus' next move.

Lazarus' gaze swept down Noir's body again. This time, lust showed in his eyes. "I'm not sure yet. Maybe if I killed you, then I could stay away."

A bark of laughter burst from Noir. "Oof. I bet that lie stung like hell."

A sexy smile exploded across Lazarus' face. "Spend the day with me."

"I am."

Lazarus gave him a sharp nod and picked up his fork. They ate in companionable silence. It was oddly nice.

God, Lazarus wished he had been lying. Noir was right. That confession had stung his pride. He had woken with Noir on his brain and had been incapable of staying away. It had only taken one call to find his address. It had taken less than that slight effort to slip past Noir's security. The guy's guard was good. Lazarus was better. He was also motivated.

"I'd offer to give you a tour of the place, but you already think I'm conceited."

Lazarus followed on Noir's heels inside. He felt every eye upon them. "All I really need to know is where to find your bedroom."

"Hmm."

Lazarus' brow furrowed. "What was that?"

Noir paused in the middle of the sitting room and turned. "I'm merely wondering if that's all you have going for you."

Lazarus' pride pricked. He stepped forward and snagged the two halves of Noir's robe, hauling him against him. Lazarus felt the mood shift in the room. The guards went on alert. He wondered for a moment how Noir lived like this. Lazarus forced himself to stay focused completely on Noir. "You didn't seem to mind last night."

Noir's gorgeous light gaze moved over Lazarus' face. His expression stayed closed, making him impossible to read. Lazarus hated that. "I maybe got carried away last night."

Lazarus untied Noir's robe. He used the two halves and his body to shield Noir's nude form from the guards' eyes. Lazarus swept his gaze down Noir's body, savoring the beauty beneath his robe. "Sorry. I had to know what you have on beneath this thing. Lucky me." He re-tied the robe. "What do you do for fun?"

Noir held his stare and didn't respond.

Lazarus had a bad feeling he was debating if he should toss Lazarus out.

He couldn't have that. Lazarus touched his lips to Noir's. He kept the kiss sweet, only slightly sucking Noir's bottom lip while holding his face between his hands. Unfortunately, he got the impression the kiss affected him more than Noir. Something stirred in his chest. When he pulled away, Noir simply turned, leaving Lazarus to follow.

"Come on. I'll show you my playroom."

He doubted Noir meant any type of sexual play area. Lazarus was right. Noir led him to a theater with every game system imaginable, along with a computer that could probably hack anything. "So, you game all day?"

Noir looked his way with a furrowed brow. "No." He moved to the computer and sat. Noir fired it to life. After a few clicks, he grabbed a nearby tablet and pen. The screen lit up with some truly badass fantasy art. After Noir made a few swipes on the tablet, it dawned on Lazarus. Noir had drawn the piece.

Lazarus sat next to him. "Damn. You did this?"

Noir nodded, but kept his gaze on the tablet. "I'm not completely useless. This is a commissioned piece for an anime series."

"That's amazing." Lazarus eyed the tablet. He was truly impressed.

Noir clicked something and images flipped across the screen—like reading a picture book.

Lazarus was fascinated. He couldn't look away. A thought creeped in. Lazarus had treated Noir like a lazy, spoiled rich boy who did nothing all day. In fact, he was a royal and still fucking worked, while Lazarus only took the occasional hit job. Which of them was lazy? He definitely knew which of them was the most judgmental. There was more to Noir than met the eye.

"Is any of this in print?"

"Sure." Noir stood. "This way."

For once, Noir didn't sound cold and distant. He sounded like a normal person. Lazarus wanted more. He followed Noir down the hall and through another door. It was a library. The shelves were stuffed with books. Lazarus looked around while Noir headed for a nearby bookcase.

"Do you read or is this just for show?"

Noir didn't look around. "I've read every book here." He handed Lazarus a book. It was almost like a comic book, but smaller and much thicker. "Here's one."

Lazarus' mind reeled as he flipped through the pages. Each image accompanied a story. He couldn't believe Noir had read every book there. There had to be thousands. Lazarus checked the copyright page to see what name Noir used for his illustrations. No way did the guy work under his real name. N.R. Stalker. Lazarus nearly snorted at the name until he noticed the author was also N.R. Stalker. His chin shot up. "You wrote this?"

Noir remained expressionless. He nodded.

It hit Lazarus. Noir had likely been schooled to always hide his emotions. He couldn't land his family on the news. Noir had to be stoic and invisible. Chances were good he used that training to keep from getting hurt.

He had exposed himself to Lazarus with this secret. That made Lazarus feel something.

Lazarus went back to checking out the pictures. "How many of these have you done?"

Noir stepped aside and motioned toward the shelf. The bookcase was filled with similar-looking books. "It's a series, following a dragon shifter throughout his life." Noir hesitated. "He's a prince who fights in his family's militia, going against other dragon sects trying to take over their land. There're fifty-two so far."

Lazarus had never been more impressed by anyone. He couldn't imagine how much time it took to write and draw the entirety of that many stories. "You're very talented. I bet you make your parents proud."

"They don't know." Noir took the book from Lazarus and put it back on the shelf. "I was sent here to be a symbol of trust, unity, and alliance with the United States. It is my duty to always foster and uphold my country's reputation and relationship with your country. My wants do not factor, nor does anyone care. I do my bi-yearly return home for TV's sake on holidays. Otherwise, I'm just here." He motioned toward the shelf. "Doing this."

Lazarus experienced an emotion he never had. Guilt. Just like everyone, Lazarus hadn't noticed the real Noir. Lazarus had less excuse than anyone. He was a watcher. A hunter. His life and freedom depended upon his ability to read people. He couldn't read Noir. Maybe that was what fascinated him so much.

"I was serious about spending the day together. Do you want to show me how that drawing tablet thing works?"

A hint of a smile touched Noir's lips. "I'd love to."

Oddly, Lazarus would too. He had come here for the off-the-charts sex. Now he couldn't wait to hear about a tablet he cared absolutely nothing about. He just wanted to be with Noir.

CHAPTER FOUR

THE AIR WAS THICK. Heavy. Lazarus explored Noir's mouth like he had nowhere to be. It had taken nothing to strip him of only a robe. Other than losing his shirt, Lazarus hadn't gotten in a hurry to go further. If he had ever made out like a teenager, Lazarus couldn't recall it. Noir made sexy sounds and writhed beneath him. Lazarus didn't ease him. The sadistic side of him needed Noir to suffer for him.

To his shock, Lazarus found himself on his back. It seemed Noir was stronger than

Lazarus thought. He started to take back control, but Noir's mouth was already headed south, and Lazarus was enthralled. Noir unbuttoned and unzipped Lazarus' jeans. Lazarus let him finish stripping him. The moment they were both nude, Lazarus' cock was in Noir's mouth and Lazarus couldn't move. Lazarus always fucked and ran, if he touched anyone at all. He didn't like feeling vulnerable and showing weakness. Getting blown was way too personal. It gave another person too much power over him. With Noir, he genuinely couldn't move a muscle. He wanted to shove him away. Lazarus had warning bells clanging in his head, but he remained completely frozen. He stared down the line of his body. Every muscle was flexed, as if he meant to spring from the bed. He couldn't look away from Noir pleasuring him.

Noir's gaze met his. He stroked Lazarus' stomach. "Relax."

Lazarus couldn't. Yet, Noir's mouth felt so fucking good. Amazing, actually. Lazarus was under his spell. He swallowed Lazarus' erection. A deep moan rumbled from Lazarus. Without realizing it, his eyes slipped closed. His muscles relaxed. Lazarus' hips lifted. He savored every sensation. His guard dropped. Noir was completely inside his head and under his skin. Lazarus forgot to protect himself. Anyone could have slit his throat in that moment and Lazarus couldn't manage to care. All he felt was the way Noir's hot mouth consumed him, sucking him toward the edge.

Noir used his hands and saliva against Lazarus. He toyed with Lazarus' balls and stroked him as he suckled Lazarus' crown. Fuck, he couldn't breathe. He sucked air and felt. Lazarus felt everything. The pressure climbing his shaft had him grabbing Noir's hair. He wanted to take his pleasure, but he couldn't bring himself to tug. He simply held on while Noir controlled him. The pressure beat at his crown. Lazarus' muscles tensed. A half second before he flew apart, Lazarus realized he hadn't pleased Noir. He shook from the power of his orgasm while Noir licked him dry. His mind was a mess. It didn't immediately return to his normal ironclad control. He hadn't made Noir come. Lazarus hadn't completed the job. Everything went haywire inside his brain. He had to finish what he started. Lazarus wanted to lash out. He fought the urge to come unglued and smash things. Things were incomplete.

Noir held his face between his hands. He looked softer than Lazarus had ever seen him. "It's okay. Take a breath. Look at me. Just breathe."

Lazarus drew a sharp breath. His lungs burned like they hadn't been used in a while. The room came a little more into focus.

Noir stroked his face. "That's it. Keep breathing. The night isn't over yet. I'd never let you leave this bed without finishing the job."

Horror overcame him. He had said those things out loud. It had been years since he had a meltdown like that. He usually stayed locked down. Lazarus knew how to keep himself in check. It was Noir. Something about him made Lazarus weak. He took him back to childhood when Lazarus couldn't control the outburst. They had been the thing that destroyed his life. Each one had gotten him beaten and locked in his room. Eventually, his parents had simply driven him into the middle of nowhere and left him. He was crazy. They couldn't afford to fix him, and he scared them. Lazarus scared himself.

His heartbeat slowed. Lazarus' mind fully cleared. Noir held him. Lazarus' throat unexpectedly swelled. He didn't... goddamn it. Lazarus didn't know how to handle the emotions suddenly crushing him, but the job still wasn't complete. Lazarus gently rolled Noir onto his back. He slowly straddled him—in case Noir was completely terrified of him now. He wanted to give Noir time to say no. Noir stared up at him, looking like he cared, and like he still wanted Lazarus. The entire situation had him completely fucked up. Yet Lazarus couldn't stop himself from covering Noir's mouth with his. Their tongues brushed. It was sweet. This kiss was unlike anything he had ever shared with anyone. He moved against Noir, trapping the man's erection between their bodies. He rolled his abs, using his strength against Noir and the friction to draw a shaky breath from Noir. Lazarus calmed a little more. He was still in control. There was still time to salvage things.

Their kiss turned more heated. Desperate. Tiny mewling sounds came from Noir as Lazarus made love to him. That was exactly what it felt like. Lazarus couldn't stop this any more than he could have stopped that blow job. Noir was different from everyone else. Lazarus didn't understand quite how yet, but he was special. For once in his life, Lazarus wanted someone's time. He craved Noir's entire focus. Lazarus wanted to own him. Possess him. Consume him. He felt insane at the idea of anyone else touching him. Lazarus was in trouble, and he couldn't stop.

Noir's breathing turned ragged. Lazarus worked harder at pleasing him. Noir's fingertips dug into Lazarus' back. The newly unleashed, possessive beast inside him roared with pleasure. He had Noir on the edge. Lazarus hadn't let him down. Noir tore his mouth away and visibly fought for air. Lazarus studied his features, ensuring he gave Noir exactly what he needed. When Noir finally blew, creating a swamp of cum between them, Lazarus recognized the truth. He wanted Noir. Not just for the night, but for good.

Noir always found peace in drawing. Life slipped away as he brought the story inside his head to life. He had never slept well. Noir assumed it was because he had no limits on his schedule. He could sleep eighteen hours or not at all. Maybe he had slept so much over the years, he wasn't tired anymore. Whatever the reason, rest eluded him. With his legs crossed and his feet tucked beneath his thighs, Noir's forearms rested on a throw pillow while he swiped his electronic pen across the screen. He had always loved dragons. When he was small, he had a nanny who read to him constantly. He never tired of disappearing into a fictional world. Noir was a thousand percent certain he had been born to create stories for other people. Unfortunately, creative people were often completely insane. That trait hadn't missed him. If he didn't make peace for himself, there was none.

Noir's eyes slipped closed as strong hands squeezed his shoulders and massaged. Lazarus' hands felt fucking amazing on Noir's body. No matter where he put them.

"How long have you been sitting here?" Lazarus' lips touched his nape.

"I don't know. After you fell asleep, I lasted about an hour before I gave up. It's not uncommon. I don't sleep well."

"You know that's a sign of a heavy conscience."

Noir couldn't stop smiling. "I see you're awake too."

A sexy chuckle vibrated against his skin. "Theory disproven then." Lazarus circled the loveseat and joined him. He crowded Noir's space and eyed the drawing. "I'm awed by you. How did you get into this, anyhow?"

Noir shrugged. "I'm the youngest and there's quite an age gap between my older brothers and me, so I was always alone. Obviously, I didn't attend public school, so there was literally no one but me. I had to have a big imagination. Thankfully, there were books and art. My parents were more than happy to hire whoever was needed to hone whatever skills I have. As long as they didn't have to interact with me, they were good."

"Sounds lonely."

Noir shrugged again. "I'm a pretty big introvert anyhow, so it's whatever. What about you? What was your childhood like?"

Lazarus didn't answer right away. Noir continued drawing while silence swelled. He didn't want to look at Lazarus and make him feel uncomfortable or judged. Either he answered or he didn't. It truly didn't matter. Finally, Lazarus cleared his throat. "It was a lot of what happened to me earlier until my parents gave up and dumped me in the woods. I mean, that didn't stop the meltdowns, but I was no longer their problem."

Noir focused on Lazarus. "Your parents abandoned you for being autistic."

Lazarus blinked. He looked confused.

The truth washed over Noir. He didn't recognize he was autistic. Noir scrambled to fix it. "Don't listen to me. It's not like I'm a doctor. I shouldn't have assumed."

Lazarus shook his head. "You're good. I just hadn't considered that, but that makes sense. In fact, it makes a lot of things clearer. Huh." Lazarus looked thoughtful for a moment. "Oh, well. I guess I figured out how to cope on my own." A smile exploded across his face. "Maybe not healthily."

Noir chuckled. He genuinely enjoyed just being with Lazarus. That never happened to him. "So, what happened after your parents dumped you in the woods? Were you raised by wolves?"

"In a manner of speaking. Turned out I wasn't as much in the middle of nowhere as my parents thought. There was a cabin owned by a rowdy bunch of bikers nearby.

It didn't take long for one to find me when he stumbled into the bushes to take a leak."

"That's wild."

Lazarus shrugged. "It was a long time ago, obviously. I'm old now," he added with a chuckle.

Noir smiled. He never smiled, but he swore he never stopped with Lazarus. "You don't look old to me."

"Mmm. I know flattery when I hear it."

Noir set his tablet aside and straddled Lazarus' lap. He ran his hands down Lazarus' bare chest. "You don't feel old to me."

The heat and humor in Lazarus' eyes had something stirring in Noir's chest. Lazarus wrapped his arms around Noir and stood, leaving Noir no other choice but to wrap his legs around him. Lazarus headed back to bed. "It's time to sleep. You need rest."

Noir wanted to argue, but it felt too good in Lazarus' arms. He had no idea where all this was headed, but he wanted as much as he could get. Noir had never been this happy. He didn't even know what to do with it.

Chapter Five

Noir: *I think this is by far the most tedious meeting with solicitors I've ever endured.*

Lazarus: *Want me to send you nudes?*

Noir: *Always.*

Lazarus: *Leaving the doctor's office now. See you soon.*

Noir: *I'm an impatient child. What did you learn?*

Noir: *Did you get everything from the beach house?*

Lazarus: *Yeah. I didn't have much left. Mostly toiletries I just threw those away. Unfortunately, I had to do that dumbass list of chores these short-term rentals leave. I don't know why they charge an outrageous cleaning fee if I'm the one doing the goddamn cleaning.*

Noir: *They charge cleaning fees? Leave it for them then. Fuck them.*

Lazarus: *I'm upstairs in the gym. Come join me.*

Noir: *Eww. Why?*

Lazarus: *It's literally your gym and you're saying eww. I want a kiss.*

Noir: *Sigh. Just a kiss?*

Lazarus: *Maybe.*

Noir: *I'll be there in a minute.*

Lazarus didn't leave the next day or the next. He dipped out a few times for errands and to grab his stuff from the beach house, but he kept returning to Noir. When Noir had meetings, Lazarus made himself scarce. The way his guards closed ranks around those meetings let Lazarus know exactly how important they were. He assumed they were royal business, and he wasn't interested in politics. It was no wonder Noir had looked so fucking bored when they met. Lazarus couldn't think of anything worse than attending those sessions.

All of Noir's free time went to Lazarus. Even when he worked on his books, he did so with his feet in Lazarus' lap. Lazarus was content with those quiet times together. He had never felt this at peace. For the first time, he no longer cared about the hunt. He had been in town for nearly a year for a mystery he hadn't thought about in months. Life was all about what kept him here now.

Noir drew.

Lazarus read. He had picked up the first book in the series, hoping to get some insight into Noir's mind. Now he couldn't stop. With one hand, he rubbed Noir's foot. He held the book with the other, engrossed. He paused and glanced Noir's way to find him quietly watching him. A smile immediately snapped to his lips.

"What?"

Noir shrugged. "Just enjoying the show."

Lazarus set his book aside. "What kind of show would you like? I'll entertain you."

Noir laughed.

Lazarus loved that sound because he knew no one else ever heard it. They were different together. There was something between them that was just for the two of them. He shifted to his knees and crawled up Noir's body. "I'll do anything you want."

Noir's eyes flashed with interest. "Anything?" He snagged Lazarus' shirt and hauled him down. Their lips met.

"Pardon the interruption, Your Highness. It's time to dress for tonight's dinner party."

Noir groaned. "Fuck. I forgot." He looked defeated. "Are you sure you don't want to go with me?"

Lazarus shuddered at the idea of wearing a tux to a country club and surrounding himself with dignitaries. "I don't clean up well. I'm more than happy to watch you dress, though." He waggled his eyebrows.

Noir didn't smile like he hoped. His gaze moved over Lazarus' face, looking concerned. "You know I'm not ashamed to be seen with you, right? I'd proudly walk in there with you tonight."

Yeah. There was definitely something here. Noir wanted to be with him as much as

Lazarus wanted to be here. In the end, they were still from two different worlds. Lazarus would never belong in Noir's sphere. "I know. Don't worry about me. I should get some shit done I've been avoiding. Enjoy your dinner. I'll be here when you get home."

"Okay."

A wicked smile lit Lazarus' face. "One kiss, though, before you leave."

"No." Noir laughed and shoved his way out from underneath Lazarus. "I know your 'just one kiss' trick. This isn't something I can be late to."

Lazarus shot to his feet and chased Noir to the bedroom. Guards tried to pretend they didn't watch as they passed. Lazarus overcame him just inside the bedroom. With his arms wrapped around Noir's waist, he hauled Noir back, holding him against his chest. He squeezed. His lips found Noir's temple.

"Behave while you're gone. No flirting with any of these rich dicks."

Noir relaxed into his hold. "What about you? Will you be out flirting with some biker dude?"

"Dude." Lazarus chuckled. "That sounded wrong in your accent. You have nothing to worry about." Noir's body felt too good against him. He took a step back. "But I'm definitely going to bounce. You're too tempting and you're about to be nude. I can't promise I'll behave with you."

"Fair." Noir moved as if he meant to leave Lazarus behind.

"Nope. Not so fast." Lazarus snagged his shirt. This time, he spun Noir in his arms and claimed his mouth. He savored every second of the way their tongues played. Lazarus breathed his air. He turned away and headed out without looking back. Lazarus hadn't been joking. Noir was too much temptation. He had to put some distance between them.

As he headed for the door to the garage, someone handed him his helmet. "Good day, sir."

Lazarus nodded. He hadn't learned everyone's names yet. Lazarus still wasn't sure if he should bother. His home was still in Arizona. Noir was still leagues above him. But goddamn it. Sometime, in the past few months of staying here, Lazarus had gotten attached. It was stupid. But after Noir's observation, Lazarus had sought a doctor's opinion. He knew it didn't really matter at this point in his life, but Noir was right. Lazarus was autistic. That realization had led to a million more. He wasn't incapable of getting close to anyone. There was so much more to it. A huge part of it had been his upbringing. He shielded himself from others, terrified of being made to feel the way his parents had. Noir was the healthiest relationship he had ever had in his entire life. For the first time, he wasn't scared to love someone. Someone genuinely seemed unafraid to love him back.

Unfortunately, there was an unhealthy side to things too. On Lazarus' side anyhow. Even though he brushed off tonight's dinner, it highlighted everything Lazarus could never be. No matter what Noir claimed, he couldn't walk proudly into that dinner with Lazarus. So Lazarus had to suck it up while countless men and women fawned all over Noir, begging to be in Lazarus' shoes. Lazarus wasn't sane. He didn't know how to cope with this simmering jealousy in a way that wouldn't destroy them. So Lazarus leaned into the crazy. He went straight for his storage locker, packed up his high-powered rifle, and set out to scope out the best vantage point to watch this party. He wouldn't shoot anyone. Just watch. Maybe.

The lush wooded areas surrounding the posh club had several spots for Lazarus to hide. He found one and settled in to watch for Noir's arrival. He put his eye to the scope and studied each new face. Three cars in, Lazarus went on high alert. His plans took a sharp turn. Andreas stepped from the back of a black SUV.

"Son of a bitch. There you are, you mother-fucker."

Lazarus quickly broke down his rifle and changed course. He would likely never get another chance like this one. Tonight, he would end this.

The ride to the country club was unusually quiet. Maybe it just felt that way without Lazarus' huge presence. Noir fought a smile just thinking his name. God, what had happened to his life? It had been absolute hell keeping his business dealings in the dark with Lazarus always under foot. It was worth every aggravation.

They were ridiculously alike. So much more than even Lazarus knew. Noir felt like himself in Lazarus' company. He didn't have to keep his shoulders squared and his chin up. Noir could relax and simply sink into his own world. He wasn't a prince with Lazarus. Noir was just a man, savoring the time alone he shared with his man. He was Noir's man. Noir would kill him before he shared him. That was why he had two of his guards tailing Lazarus tonight. He tried to work up an ounce of guilt, but he had no shame. Noir's jealousy was an ugly thing. He didn't want Lazarus to see it. It wasn't that he didn't trust Lazarus. They hadn't truly defined their relationship yet. That left Noir feeling like he was on shaky ground. He had no clue how to handle things in a healthy way. For now, subterfuge it was.

"I've never seen you like this."

Noir's gaze slid Ajax's way. "What way do you mean?" He knew. Noir just wanted to hear Ajax's observations.

"Happy. I can practically hear you thinking about him."

It was damn hard to keep his face expressionless. He wanted to smile and gush like an idiot. "I don't know how to respond to that. It would be unbecoming of me to admit to any sort of unhappiness."

A sad smile touched Ajax's lips. "To anyone else, maybe, but I've known you your whole life. I know your dad. Your upbringing. To anyone else, you look like you have it all. I've been right here, seeing the real you."

Noir couldn't deny it. He spent a moment measuring his words before he spoke. "He is amazing, though, right? This isn't in my head. I'm not just seeing what I want to see, am I? I've never been sure how much I can trust my mind."

"It's real. That man cares for you. Your dad will hate him."

A smile exploded across his face. "Maybe. When has that ever mattered to me?"

Ajax shook his head. "It's good to see you smile."

The car came to a stop in front of the club. Noir took a breath and arranged his features into the bored royal. Press waited, the way they always did. "His Royal Highness, Prince Noir Antonsen."

Noir stepped from the car and headed for the door. Lights flashed, and he kept his gaze straight ahead. He didn't move too fast or too slow. Noir had to look unaffected in every way. This was it. This was the thing that had him fucked in the head. He wasn't real to anyone. Why would he believe he was real himself? He could do anything. No one cared. Not only did he have diplomatic immunity, no one would dare insult a prince. This entire existence was suffocating. Yet he should be grateful for drowning. He should appreciate every breath this life stole from him. No one saw him... except maybe Lazarus did. That was where he wanted to be.

"Noir. You're looking extra annoyed tonight."

Noir accepted a glass of champagne and focused on Heath. They had known each other for years. Heath's family were the largest oil stockholders in the U.S., and he shared in the list of the top ten most eligible bachelors in Atlantic City with Noir. That fucking list. It sucked to be that wanted.

"Heath. I'm surprised you're here. Don't you usually skip these things?"

Heath's gray eyes flashed with devilry. "Well, rumor is you're dating 'gutter trash.'" Heath did the full air quotes. "Bets were made if you were brave enough to bring him tonight. I, for one, was rooting for you. What these assholes consider trash makes for the best lovers, or so I've found."

Noir was furious. He would be damned if he showed it. "I asked him to come, but he had another engagement. It's also rather funny to me these people think of a millionaire as gutter trash. I can't imagine how they must hate themselves. Most of them can't even claim that status." He knew it was wrong to expose Lazarus' wealth. Noir didn't care what people thought of him, but Lazarus didn't deserve their disdain. While he had made his money in the dirtiest way, no one made that much money ethically. That was just life. Noir also knew Heath got drunk and told everything he knew. He wouldn't hesitate to use that to his advantage.

"I hadn't heard that part. What's his trade?"

An evil smile pulled at the corners of Noir's mouth. "He's who people call when they need someone to downsize their company."

Heath nodded, looking thoughtful. "I imagine that is a lucrative field. Companies would pay a lot to have someone else face the wrath, but it's a job that must be done sometimes."

Noir nodded. Heath had no idea.

After a moment of looking around, Heath made his excuses. "I suppose I should find my table."

Noir knew he couldn't wait to spread his new piece of gossip. "Of course. It was good to see you, as always."

Heath flashed him a final smile and was off like a shot. Noir chuckled under his breath. This night might turn out to be more interesting than he expected. He never tired of stirring the pot.

CHAPTER SIX

IT DIDN'T TAKE LONG, after disposing of the driver, for Andreas to slide into the back-seat and straight into Lazarus' trap. Lazarus locked the doors as he pulled away from the club. Andreas stared at his phone, ignoring someone he no doubt felt was below him. That worked in Lazarus' favor. He waited until they were in a secluded area before switching on a signal blocker, making it impossible for Andreas to call for help.

Lazarus pulled to the shoulder of the road.

Andreas' chin shot up. He blinked at the sight of Lazarus. "Where is Gerard?"

Lazarus smiled. "He's indisposed. We need to have a conversation."

Andreas did everything Lazarus expected. He tried to make a call. When that didn't work, he tried jumping from the vehicle. The door wouldn't open. He didn't focus on Lazarus again until he recognized there was no escape. His eyes flashed with rage. "You have no idea who you're dealing with."

"Exactly." Lazarus leveled his gun at Andreas. "Who do you work for?"

Andreas looked confused. "I'm a money manager. I work for a Fortune 500 company."

Lazarus rolled his eyes. "Don't play dumb. I want to know who ordered the hit on Cutler Maine's husband."

Andreas blinked some more. "The CIA agent? No one."

Ah, he wasn't quite as oblivious as he claimed. "No one? I find that hard to believe since I found his attacker stabbed to death with a note telling us we were square. That doesn't sound like no one."

Andreas made a helpless gesture. He dropped the act of being oblivious. "I'm being genuine. No one ordered a hit. That's exactly why his attacker ended up dead. He stepped out of line. I won't be joining him by betraying anyone. Not that it matters. I know what you want and I can't give it to you. I legitimately have no idea who pulls the strings."

Lazarus' eyes narrowed. "I call bullshit. Everyone says you're second in command. You don't get that close and not know who you answer to."

Andreas leaned forward, showing an insane lack of fear. "First off, ha. I'm no one. It's my job to manage the money of several out-landishly rich men. It could be any one of them running this town. Secondly, I don't want to know. They say Rico had over a hundred stab wounds. I'm not going out like that. My job is above board and I intend to keep it that way, but you're a goddamn fool if you think anyone's money is clean. I'll be damned if I worry about where a single penny comes from that's crossed my desk."

He was convincing, but something still didn't feel right. "You're telling me you know absolutely nothing? That sounds a lot like I have no reason to keep you alive."

Andreas looked worried for the first time. Lazarus could practically see him searching his brain for any detail that might save him. "People call him the dragon. Apparently, he has a terrifying temper. I've never heard a name beyond that. If anyone knows, though, it's—"

The glass next to Lazarus exploded. Before he had time to recover and react, he was dragged from the SUV. Something thick covered his face, making it hard to breathe and impossible to see. He couldn't fight. Lazarus tried, but it was obviously more than one guy. No one made a sound. Even as Lazarus fought for his life, there was complete silence. His body slammed into a rough surface. Handcuffs clicked around his wrists, binding them behind his back. In no time, he was in a vehicle and on the move. Lazarus tried using his teeth to move the material from his head. Unfortunately, it seemed to be tied—like a sack with a drawstring around his neck. He was trapped. All Lazarus could do was wait for his chance. Then these men were dead. He didn't take prisoners.

Lazarus tried memorizing every turn. Unfortunately, he was disoriented. He lost count of turns and track of miles. Instead, Lazarus focused on surrounding sounds when he was dragged from the vehicle. He heard the ocean. Lazarus half expected to get tossed into the water and left to drown. Instead, the sound drowned away as a door opened and closed. There were no unfamiliar sounds or smells. They headed down—possibly to a basement or storeroom. He didn't struggle. Lazarus needed to conserve his energy. He was bound to a chair. Either the torture would start soon, or his abductors would reveal themselves. Either way, he needed his strength. Lazarus had to get home to Noir. He couldn't let him down.

Ajax didn't join Noir's driver to pick him up. Noir was grateful for the quiet. He had a pounding headache and just wanted to get home to Lazarus. As always at these events, the food had been too heavy and the conversation shallow. Noir wanted to take a shower and curl up in Lazarus' arms. These events weren't often, but thcy wcrc draining. He needed Lazarus to soothe him. Noir's life left him mentally exhausted. He had to get back to his happy place.

Noir stepped inside to find the house quiet as the dead of night. Ajax appeared in an instant.

"We have a problem."

A sick feeling settled in Noir's gut. Had his worst fears been true? Did his guards catch

Lazarus cheating? A pain sliced across his chest. He couldn't handle that. Ajax's dour expression had his heart rate kicking into high gear. He took a breath. "Tell me." Even he heard the exhaustion in his voice.

"Emil and Bendt followed Lazarus, as you requested." Noir's throat swelled. It was his nightmare coming to life. "He kidnapped Andreas and questioned him." It was sad how relieved he was. "Obviously, Andreas would never betray you, but the men were forced to intervene to prevent Lazarus from killing our top guy."

Oh no. A lump rose in his throat. "What did they do?" There was no missing the barely suppressed rage in his voice.

Ajax motioned for Noir to follow. They headed downstairs. Emil and Bendt stood off to the side, looking like they feared Noir's wrath, as they should. In the center of the room, Lazarus was bound to a chair with his head covered. His chin lifted as Noir stepped fully into the room, almost as if he recognized Noir's footfalls.

Noir swallowed the bile rising in his throat and hardened his heart. Ajax dragged a chair across from Lazarus for Noir to sit. Noir sat and stared at Lazarus. There had never been any chance of avoiding this forever. Noir took a breath and gave Ajax a sharp nod.

Ajax ripped the hood from Lazarus.

Lazarus looked furious until he fully focused on Noir. His fury turned to open confusion. Noir watched his expression shift through every emotion before hitting realization and stopping at barely suppressed rage.

Noir motioned for the guards to leave them. No one questioned his order. Everyone knew he was the most dangerous person there.

Noir took another deep breath. "I didn't order a hit on your friend." That part was important. No matter what else happened, Noir needed Lazarus to know that much.

"So I've been told."

It seemed Andreas hadn't been completely silent. Noir supposed he was grateful in a way. But Noir fucking hated how cold Lazarus sounded. He didn't know how to make Lazarus understand.

"Who killed Rico?"

At least Lazarus' curiosity kept him from completely shutting down. "I did. He stepped out of line all because he thought with his dick and let the CIA get the drop on him. His pride killed him."

"You did that?"

Even though Lazarus' voice remained cold, he sounded disbelieving. At least they were talking. Noir would take it. "I don't send people to do my dirty work. If I want someone dead, then I should be man enough to handle it."

"You knew I was hunting you. Was all this..." Lazarus didn't finish. It was like he couldn't say the words. Noir got it. He imagined this entire relationship looked like a way to shut him down. Noir would suspect the same in his shoes.

His life was something he had never been able to explain. Noir knew he had to try now, or he would lose Lazarus. "Imagine from the first day you're born, there's nothing out of your reach. In fact, you don't even have to ask. Your every desire is anticipated. One day, you suddenly realize you're nothing. There's nothing. Life is totally meaningless. Pointless. I think that was the rock bottom my father waited for me to hit. He wanted me to do everything a million times until I hated it. That's when he struck. How would I like to be the iron fist of our country in the U.S.? No risk. I have immunity here. No one would even suspect me. I could syphon an endless supply of money from this country into ours while keeping as much as I liked. He offered me power I would never have back home, considering my place in the line of succession. Back home, I would always be a useless prince. Here, I could be a king. My hands no less dirty than running a kingdom. How could I say no? I couldn't suffocate another day."

Noir swallowed because that wasn't where the story ended. "Except, eventually, I realized I was still nothing. The only time I didn't feel crushed beneath the weight of... I don't even know how to describe it. No one seeing me. Being just the subject of a headline. I don't exist unless I'm working on my books." Noir held Lazarus' stare. "And when I'm with you. You see me. I'm real to you."

"Imagine if you hadn't lied to me."

Noir's eyes fell closed at Lazarus' words. He stood. Noir fully intended to immediately release Lazarus and face the music. Instead, he straddled Lazarus' lap. He couldn't stop himself. Noir held Lazarus' face between his hands. He touched his lips to Lazarus' mouth. Noir half expected Lazarus to bite him or head butt him. He didn't. Lazarus opened for him, kissing him back. It was sweet. Their kiss felt like goodbye. Noir pulled away and pressed his forehead against Lazarus's. He squeezed his eyes shut, absorbing a final moment. Sharing a final breath. "I know it doesn't matter now, but I love you." Noir stood and headed for the stairs. He didn't look back. "I'll send Ajax to set you free. I'm sorry you were inconvenienced." Noir didn't know if he meant tonight or for the entirety of their relation-ship. Probably both. He would go back to being invisible. Noir was toxic. This was best for everyone.

CHAPTER SEVEN

IF NOIR THOUGHT LIFE was empty before Lazarus, it was nothing compared to after he walked out. Sometimes, Noir would turn sideways while drawing, expecting his feet to land on Lazarus' lap. The heartbreak would hit all over again from just a moment of forgetfulness. Other times, the anger would try to creep in. Noir hadn't shunned Lazarus for his line of work. Each time those moments came, Noir had to remind himself Lazarus had never hidden himself. From night one, he had been completely honest, letting Noir choose to stay. Hell, maybe Lazarus saw drugs as worse than murder. Then again, he had killed people too. He was no prize. Not really.

Such a short few months shouldn't have affected him the way they had, but when a person had never experienced real love, it was addictive. It was impossible to not become a sponge, soaking up everything life had withheld. Each day that passed, Noir felt himself losing more of the warmth Lazarus had brought into his life. Soon, he would be completely cold again.

"You have a visitor, Your Highness."

Noir glanced over his shoulder.

Heath stood in the doorway. He was all smiles. "Are you seriously still sitting in your robe at two in the afternoon?"

Noir didn't experience an ounce of guilt. He had no reason to dress. "I have nowhere to be."

Heath crossed the room and claimed the spot beside him on the loveseat. Lazarus' spot. "I truly expected to find your man relaxing at your feet."

"I'm not sure you can call him my man, since I haven't heard from him in three weeks."

Heath stretched his legs out, settling in like he lived there. "Did you self-destruct?"

That was a fair question. Maybe—in a way—he had. "It's possible. I can't tell any longer."

Heath slapped Noir's knee and squeezed. "Get dressed. We're going to the country club. We can get some drinks and socialize. Get out of your fucking robe, for fuck's sake. This isn't good for your mental health."

Noir bit back a groan. "I hate the club. Everyone stares at me like I'm part of a menagerie—like I'm not a real person. Now that's not good for my mental health."

Heath met his stare. He looked more serious than Noir had ever seen. "No one is real."

Noir held his breath. It was the first time he heard anyone in his circle admit to feeling like him.

A sad smile touched Heath's lips. "That's the big secret. We're all just putting on a show together, dancing to a silent tune. The only thing you can do is put on the best goddamn act anyone has ever seen. Win the mother fucking best actor of the year award. But whatever you do, don't disappear into your head. You're not beating the game. You're just losing your soul. Go get dressed. If you don't want to go to the country club, we'll find a nightclub and get lost in a crowd. But you're not staying here and drowning."

Noir swallowed. He genuinely didn't want to go anywhere, but Heath was right. Noir felt himself slipping away to a place of no return. So he had lost the only person who truly knew him to his core. There had never been much of a chance Noir could hang on to him. Lazarus had given him five beautiful months. Noir would treasure the memories, but it was time to accept his role. Noir had been born to be nothing but a symbol—untouchable. Only a face. He knew his place. It was time for Noir to accept he was cursed to be alone. That was how it would always be.

Air ruffled Lazarus' hair. He rode through the streets, trying not to think or feel. His home in Arizona still waited for him. He wasn't sure why he hadn't returned yet. His work was done here. There was no mystery to solve or grand villain to slay. Lazarus should go home, polish his weapons, and await his next job. There was always someone who needed killing. This wasn't his town. He had no idea why he stayed.

His phone buzzed. Lazarus slowed. No one knew his number unless he gave it to them. His phone was encrypted and didn't exist on paper. There was no trail to follow to find it. An incoming text likely meant a new target. Lazarus pulled into the first empty parking lot he came to. With his feet braced, keeping the bike balanced, Lazarus took his phone from his pocket and checked his message. It was a blocked number. He opened it and an image appeared on the screen. Noir lounged against a bar next to a young, and objectively sexy guy. The man was probably the same age as Noir. Noir wore his typical bored royal expression. The guy next to him, talking close to Noir's ear, was all smiles. The dude looked like a player. Lazarus didn't see him, though. He couldn't tear his gaze away from Noir. His eyes looked dead. The light had left him. Lazarus dropped his gaze to the text attached to the image.

Blocked number: *Come get your man before someone else does.*

Lazarus couldn't begin to guess who sent the message. All he knew was he couldn't do this anymore. Lazarus couldn't keep telling himself he had never really known Noir. He knew him. They knew each other. Lazarus had always recognized the crazy in Noir's eyes. It had been like looking in a mirror. Likely, they were the only two people on the planet who understood them. Lazarus would be goddamned if some young buck swooped in and took his place. The more he thought about things, the more furious he became. Noir had a lot of fucking nerve. He had told Lazarus he loved him, yet he was out with someone else. Noir should damn well know Lazarus could never leave him. Lazarus was angry, but he would never completely walk away. He couldn't. Noir was an addiction. He focused on the image again and let the rage build. The anger fed him. Noir looked broken. How dare he?

Lazarus shoved the phone back inside his pocket. He tore from the parking lot. Lazarus didn't need to call around to find Noir. He had stolen Noir's phone and shared the guy's location with himself a long time ago. Lazarus would never let him get away. It took him less than ten minutes to tear into the parking lot of an exclusive bar. There wasn't a car in the lot under a hundred thousand. He barely had his bike parked before he was headed for the door. The doormen exchanged a glance at Lazarus' aggressive approach. It was obvious they had never dealt with anyone like him.

Lazarus ripped open the door.

"Sir, this is a members-only establishment."

"And we have a dress code," the second guy added—like it mattered since he didn't have a membership.

All eyes turned his way as Lazarus stormed inside. The music didn't exactly screech to a halt, but literally everyone froze at the sight of him. Even though Lazarus wore leather boots and pants along with a sleeveless shirt, he didn't for one second think that was why he had stunned the crowd into silence. Lazarus felt murderous. He couldn't even begin to imagine how he looked. Yet the two pesky doormen still kept trying to shoo him out. There were some vague threats about the police. Lazarus didn't truly hear a word. His full focus was on Noir. Like everyone, Noir's gaze was locked on him. Unlike everyone else, he didn't look afraid.

Lazarus pushed a doorman aside and ate up the distance between Noir and him. Noir didn't flinch or run. Lazarus grabbed two handfuls of Noir's shirt and hauled him forward. He went nose to nose with him, ensuring Noir saw the truth in his eyes.

"You're mine." His mouth slammed down on Noir's so hard, he tasted blood. He devoured Noir, taking the kiss he was owed.

"Can he do that? Can someone just kiss a prince?"

The whispered words were the first to penetrate his rage.

Noir chuckled against his lips. His arms encircled Lazarus' neck.

Lazarus pulled away and pressed his forehead against Noir's, holding his stare. "I see you. None of these fucking people see you. I do. You are real to me. How dare you come here with someone else?"

Noir kissed him, killing the last of Lazarus' rage.

"Sir, for the last time, we seriously have to ask you to leave."

Noir pulled away and leveled a cold stare at the doorman. "Are you seriously accosting my guest right now?"

The guy floundered like a fish. His mouth opened and closed several times before finally finding his voice. "Of course not, Prince Noir. It's just—"

At the man's audacity to approach Noir, Noir's guards closed ranks, blocking anyone's access to get close enough to speak. They turned their backs on Lazarus and

Noir, hiding them from sight and keeping them safe. Giving them privacy.

Noir stroked Lazarus' face and chest. "I can't believe you're here. You shut me out. I didn't think I'd see you again." He stole a sweet kiss. "I'm so goddamn sorry, Lazarus."

Lazarus covered Noir's mouth with his, cutting off that nonsense. He held Noir's face gently between his hands, treasuring him. "Stop. I love you. Please stop."

Noir held his stare, looking shocked. "What?"

"You heard me. Let's go. We have shit to talk about." He didn't wait for Noir to agree. Lazarus stooped, grabbed Noir, and tossed him over his shoulder.

"Did he just toss a prince over his shoulder? No way this is happening right now."

Noir pressed his face against Lazarus' back and laughed.

Lazarus couldn't stop smiling on the way to the door. Like a well-oiled machine, Noir's royal guard stayed tight knit around them, all the way out the door. Lazarus never looked to see what became of the boy trying to take his place. That guy didn't matter. No one did. Noir belonged to Lazarus. It was time Noir understood it.

CHAPTER EIGHT

HEATH WATCHED NOIR GET carried from the club while sipping his drink. He imagined another highly sought after bachelor would soon disappear from the elite's most eligible. It was a pity. They seemed to drop like flies lately.

"Well, that was embarrassing."

Heath glanced over at the dryly spoken statement. He blinked. The most beautiful man he had ever seen stood nearby. Still, Heath liked to think of himself as a romantic deep, deep down. "I don't know. I think it was a little sweet."

The guy's mouth lifted in one corner. "I meant for you. Wasn't that your date?"

Heath snorted. "I don't care about anyone enough to let them humiliate me."

"Oh, yes. The typical bored rich daddy's boy. Sad."

Heath's hint of irritation turned into true aggravation. "Ah, a jealous nobody, hanging out looking for their next sugar daddy. I should've known. Just a pretty face." If the guy wanted to get catty, Heath would oblige. He had all night.

"Are you ready, Court?"

The guy glanced over at the inquiry. A smooth smile touched his lips. "Of course." He accepted the arm of a man Heath had seen hundreds of times. Portland was the

CEO of the top bank on the east coast. He nodded at Heath as he passed, moving to the door with Heath's antagonizer. Court glanced over his shoulder and smirked. Heath fumed. Asshole pretty boy. Heath didn't need anyone. He cared not at all what some gold-digging hussy thought of him. Heath had no idea why he couldn't stop grinding his back teeth. He didn't care about anyone.

Showing no regard for his guards, as always, Lazarus refused to let Noir out of his sight long enough to get home. He put Noir on his bike and drove him home himself. Noir couldn't stop touching him. He couldn't believe he was real. Noir had never expected to set eyes on him again.

At the house, once again, Lazarus didn't give him a chance to get away. Not that he would. Lazarus snatched Noir off his feet and stormed inside. His jaw worked double time—like he was still pissed. Noir didn't quite understand his anger, but he didn't care. He would take any version of Lazarus he could get.

Lazarus headed straight for their private sitting room inside their bedroom. Noir didn't even blink at his thoughts. It was their room. Ajax was hot on their heels. Noir didn't miss the way he hid a smile. Ajax veered to the left, taking up his spot outside the door. Lazarus sat on the loveseat, cradling Noir in his arms. He stared straight ahead—like he feared himself. Noir tried to wait him out.

He failed. "You didn't give me the chance earlier to say I love you too."

Lazarus' chin finally dropped. The way his eyes burned with emotion had Noir's throat swelling. "Why? I don't deserve it."

That confused the fuck out of Noir. "Why would you say that? Of course you do."

Lazarus swallowed so hard, it had to hurt. "I left when you stayed. You never judged me or questioned where I went when we weren't together. You never questioned me. From day one, you accepted me. I don't deserve it."

Noir shifted positions, straddling Lazarus' lap. He ran his hands up Lazarus' chest until his fingers linked behind Lazarus' neck. His gaze never wavered from holding Lazarus' stare. "It's not the same. I know why you left, and I didn't blame you. You showed a trust in me I didn't return by confiding in you. I wanted to tell you, but I was scared to lose you because you're right. None of these mother fuckers see me. You and I were meant to meet. I believe that. You have no idea how much I wish I had trusted in that and been truthful. I was just scared." Noir knew he was just repeating himself at this point, but he needed Lazarus to understand. He had feared nothing like he did losing Lazarus.

Lazarus cupped his face like Noir was precious to him. Noir didn't miss the way his hands shook. "You were out with someone else."

Noir turned his head and kissed Lazarus' wrist. He met Lazarus' stare again. "None of these mother fuckers see me," he repeated, incapable of bringing his voice above a whisper. Everything hurt without Lazarus. He hated this weakness, but he couldn't stop it. Lazarus had wormed his way into Noir's soul. He was invisible without him.

Lazarus stood and headed for the bed. He never let go of Noir. Noir held on and held Lazarus' stare. Neither of them broke the connection. They were equally intense people. Together, they were explosive and a tad unstable. Noir couldn't imagine anyone else touching him. Lazarus crawled onto the bed, covering Noir's body with his. Noir's heart hummed. His cock throbbed. He knew what Lazarus could and would do to him. Lazarus was methodical. Like always, he studied Noir's every reaction as he stripped him.

"No one else is allowed to touch you."

Noir nodded. "I know."

"No one else will ever touch me."

Jealousy and rage flared to life in Noir's chest. "I know." Even he heard the deadly bite to his words.

For a moment, Lazarus froze. He eyed Noir, seeing something only he knew. Finally, he smiled. "God, it's so fucking hot knowing you'd actually kill for me."

He would. Noir pulled Lazarus down and took the kiss he wanted. Lazarus had come back to him. There was no escaping him now. If anyone thought to take him, they were dead.

Everything inside Lazarus was lit like a firework, ready to blow. He was horny, in love, and still slightly enraged. It didn't matter that guy had been no one. It equally didn't matter Lazarus knew Noir wouldn't let anyone else touch him. Someone had sent him that picture. Whoever had taken it obviously believed Lazarus could be replaced. He had to find a way to ensure that misconception disappeared in everyone's mind. Noir would be his and only his, or he would be dead. This was until death parted them, one way or another.

He couldn't get inside Noir fast enough. Lazarus used the bare minimum of lube and prep. His patience was gone. When he shoved his way inside Noir, Noir was nude, but Lazarus still wore everything, including his boots. He froze, partially because it felt so fucking good inside Noir, and partly because he recognized how much he looked like an ass. Noir had to think he didn't care about anything except getting off. Lazarus pulled out and stripped.

Noir watched him with a heated stare.

Lazarus was back before Noir had time to cool. This time, he claimed Noir's mouth as he slipped inside. His heart squeezed. He was so in love. So fucking in love. Lazarus never dreamed he could feel this way. He understood now the way Cutler had come unglued over Gable's attack. If anyone ever hurt Noir, God help this world. He would burn the planet to the ground. No one else mattered. He rocked inside Noir, taking what he wanted while giving everything. Nothing got him hotter than pleasuring Noir. Just knowing he was the reason Noir blew was enough to keep him high. Noir was so above him, so untouchable. It never stopped amazing him that Noir let him be here.

Noir's breathing changed. He reached above him and grabbed the headboard as if needing purchase. Lazarus doubled his efforts. Noir turned desperate beneath him. Lazarus watched every nuance. He craved these moments and always seared them into his memory. Noir held his stare as he came. Something dark and doubly possessive roared to life inside him. Prince or not,

Noir would marry him. He didn't know their protocols for that. Maybe he dreamed the impossible, but it would still happen. Noir was his. There was no escape. The pressure in his cock stole his thoughts. His orgasm took him out totally. He ceased to exist anywhere except the heaven of Noir's arms. This was forever. He couldn't accept less.

CHAPTER NINE

His Majesty, King Aksel Antonsen, requests your presence at Seashire Palace at 12 p.m. on the 25th day of December. The family will gather precisely one hour beforehand for a private toast.

His name was on the invitation. Lazarus stood no chance of saying no. But Noir bought him a robe. Lazarus secretly loved it. He understood now why Noir never wanted to dress. Plus, the lack of clothing made for easier access. Lazarus did enjoy touching Noir. He desperately wished he could stay in that robe, sit by the Christmas tree, and enjoy his first normal holiday with the man he loved. Unfortunately, unlike Lazarus, Noir had a family. A royal one. What a nightmare. Lazarus ran out of random thoughts to busy his mind from the stressful situation. He was under a microscope.

Lazarus donned his coldest demeanor, using it like a shield from the obvious judgement. Somewhere, in the back of his mind, there was a tiny voice telling him he would win more flies with honey. Lazarus was overwhelmed, which always brought out the worst in him. For Noir's sake, he tried staying quiet, so he remained civil.

Noir's father, Aksel, looked so much like Noir, ridiculously so. They looked the same age. It was eerie. They could be twins, except where Noir always appeared bored, Aksel looked cold. His cool stare cut right through people. He was a king in every way. Even if Lazarus hadn't known that, he still would have known. The guy was regal. He knew he was above everyone in the room, including his son. Lazarus was less than the dirt beneath his boot.

"I hear you carried my son from a nightclub like a bag of trash."

Well, fuck. He had done that. "I did."

Aksel narrowed his eyes. "That's it? You did? No excuses?"

Lazarus refused to apologize. "I did what had to be done. He was somewhere he shouldn't be with someone he shouldn't have been with. I remedied the situation."

Not a single muscle twitched in Noir's face. He sat like a stone while Aksel stared at Lazarus with a hard expression.

Finally, Aksel snorted before roaring with laughter. He glanced Noir's way and said something in a foreign language.

Noir's eyes swam with laughter. He focused on Lazarus. "He says I should marry you now before someone else does."

Lazarus' throat swelled so hard and fast, his head swam. He didn't know if Noir laughed at the ridiculousness of the idea or if he was simply relieved by his father's reaction. Either way, Lazarus couldn't let the moment pass.

"You should."

At the seriousness of Lazarus' tone, Noir's smile fell. "Wait. Are you serious?"

Before Lazarus could answer, Aksel slapped his knees and stood. "Now isn't the time. This is a holiday. One of the very few where I get to see you. Let's eat and then open presents. I'm sure there's at least one person ready to sneak a picture of our happy family."

Noir stood and straightened his jacket, falling back into royal mode. "Of course."

Lazarus studied Noir's expression as he stood. Before heading to Noir's home country, Noir had called in his tailor to make Lazarus look as much the part as possible. Now his suit chafed, and he was overheated. His tie felt too tight, and he couldn't breathe. But still, Lazarus only had eyes for Noir. He needed to know what thoughts rattled in his head. Lazarus wanted to force Noir to tell him where they were headed. Unfortunately, Noir avoided his gaze as he headed for the formal dining room where his family's guests waited. They had already been cooling their heels for too long while Aksel met Lazarus properly and without witnesses. It had been a stressful morning. Now Lazarus had all these thoughts in his head, making insecurities grow. Maybe Noir didn't want to get married. He understood things weren't cut and dry due to Noir's position, but fuck. Lazarus was willing to do whatever it took. Surely, Noir knew that by now. That left only one conclusion. Noir didn't want this. Where the fuck was he supposed to go with that?

Noir watched Lazarus's mood blacken by the minute. His expression turned so scary, people made a wide berth. Occasionally, he would catch Noir's eye and soften a hair, but then he was back to glowering at everyone. Noir didn't know what he had done. Lazarus's mood dampened his plans. He didn't give two fucks if everyone was terrified of Lazarus. His father loved that about him. Noir loved that about him. He was sexy as hell when he looked ready to kill. Lazarus had Noir ready to rip off his clothes. He also had Noir worried. Maybe getting a firsthand look at royal life was enough to convince him this wasn't what he wanted. There was a lot of pomp and circumstance that went with major holidays. They weren't gathered around the tree with hot cocoa. Everything they did was watched and judged. Their day would be aired to the public. He thought he might hyperventilate. Noir tried hard to smile when appropriate and be stoic when it wasn't. He couldn't take his eyes off Lazarus and his barely contained temper. It felt like the day would never end. By the time they were allowed to escape to their private quarters, Noir wanted to tear off his skin. He ground his back teeth on the walk. Noir barely made it until the door closed behind them before he turned on Lazarus.

"Spill."

A line appeared between Lazarus' eyebrows. "Spill what?"

Noir peeled off his coat before making an impatient gesture. "Whatever has you trying to kill everyone with one glance. All day, you've looked ready to fly into a rage. If this is too much for you, you can say it. I know asking you to come here was asking a lot more than you likely signed up for. There are things I have no choice about. I totally get that you do. I completely understand how overwhelming this must be."

"What in the hell are you talking about? This is exactly what I signed up for. Do you think

I'm dumb? I knew loving you meant playing a part when needed."

"Then why are you so angry?"

Lazarus' chest expanded as he drew an audibly deep breath. "You don't want to marry me." The words burst from Lazarus as if he knew if he didn't just say it, then he never would. He even winced afterward, as if he hated how he sounded.

Noir blinked. "What?"

Lazarus' shoulders fell. He peeled off his jacket and tossed it on the settee next to Noir's. "It's stupid. Never mind. I love you and it shouldn't matter. It just stung a little when you reacted the way you did to your dad's joke. You obviously took it as just that: a joke." He finally met Noir's stare again. "It's not a joke to me. I love you and I want to marry you, but I get it. I'm me." He motioned toward himself. "You're you." He motioned toward Noir, as if that should explain every-thing. "You're right. I'm not good enough for this."

Noir couldn't stop blinking while his mind tried processing the complete idiocy of every word Lazarus said. "Well, fuck." Nothing ever went smoothly with them. "You're kind of fucking up my Christmas right now."

Lazarus' expression turned thunderous. "I'm sorry. You asked. If you didn't want to know how I feel, why in the fuck did you start this?"

A smile exploded across Noir's face. He really loved this ridiculously angry and abrasive man. He shook his head. "No." He held up one finger, asking Lazarus to wait. Noir grabbed his jacket and dug through the pocket. "You're ruining my plans for you for Christmas." Noir dropped to one knee and opened the ring box he had planned to give Lazarus later tonight.

Lazarus focused on the ring.

Noir didn't give him time to respond. He needed to at least get to ask properly. "I'd planned a romantic dinner tonight. You know, the whole by a roaring fire on Christmas night thing. But I won't have you walking around thinking I don't love you more than life. I can't let you believe I don't want forever with you. Will you marry me?"

Lazarus didn't respond.

A nervous laugh rumbled from Noir. "I know I'm young, but I don't really kneel for anyone, and this floor is hard. Even without bad knees, this is rough. You're allowed to say no; just do it quickly. I'd rather get bruises on my knees the fun way."

Lazarus' gaze moved from the ring to Noir's face. "You really had that in your pocket the whole time."

It wasn't a question, but Noir still nodded.

Lazarus froze again for a second before blinking again, as if he couldn't escape the shock. "I really ruined your proposal."

He hadn't been kidding about being on one knee, but Noir didn't budge. "It honestly doesn't matter how it happened, as long as you say yes."

"Yes."

Noir pushed to his feet. He hadn't truly doubted Lazarus' answer, except he worried Lazarus might be offended Noir was the one who asked. The moment felt oddly serious. Part of him wanted to smile like an idiot. The rest of him couldn't stop showing the moment the respect it deserved. Without thinking, he fell into his training, staying stoic. He slipped the ring on Lazarus's finger. It looked a little tight, but he didn't complain.

"Don't do that."

Noir's chin shot up. He couldn't handle Lazarus changing his mind.

Lazarus held his stare. "Don't be fake with me. Don't retreat behind a mask."

"I'm not. This is me promising you the world. I want you to look at me and know I mean it. This isn't me caught up in the moment with you. I'm not riding the high of love where reality will catch up later. We're real and I'm very serious. I want this."

Lazarus cupped his face and shuffled closer. "I'll never be some normal guy."

"Good." Noir had never meant anything more. He wasn't some normal guy. Why would he want that from someone else?

"I love you." Lazarus skimmed his lips across Noir's mouth. "People will think you're fucking insane for marrying me."

Noir smiled. "Good. I am insane."

Lazarus kissed him again. His lips shaped a smile against Noir's. "You're amazing."

Noir couldn't stop grinning. He had never been happier. "I love you too."

This time, Lazarus' kiss turned heated. Noir wanted to tear off his clothes. Lazarus didn't let him. The moment Noir's hands went for Lazarus' belt, Lazarus grabbed his hands and pulled away. "Not yet. You haven't gotten my gift." He headed for his toiletries bag, which still sat packed on a nearby table. Lazarus dug around until he came back with two small boxes. "I didn't want you to think I copped out with this one." He showed the smaller box. "Plus, I wasn't sure if I would give it to you yet. So I also got you this one." He shook the bigger box. They both looked like velvet jewelry boxes. "Which one would you like first?"

There was nothing Noir couldn't buy for himself, but he was oddly giddy. No one bought him gifts out of love. Whatever Lazarus had done had come from the heart. His excitement grew by the second. "Shuffle them behind your back and I'll pick a hand."

Lazarus chuckled at his childishness, but did what Noir asked.

Noir motioned toward the left. "That one."

Lazarus brought his hand around and passed Noir the bigger box.

Noir practically danced in place as he flipped it open. It was a watch. Noir was stunned. It was a beautiful piece. "Damn." He didn't know what else to say. The watch was exactly something he would've chosen for himself.

"There's an engraving on the back."

Noir took the watch from the box and flipped it over. He read the words aloud. "This is a tracking device." Noir threw his head back and roared with laughter. He couldn't stand still. He headed for the table and set the empty box aside, still chuckling. If ever there was a more Lazarus gift, Noir couldn't think of one. He put the watch on his wrist. "I'll gladly wear it, since you're already tracking my phone." Noir laughed harder at Lazarus' shocked expression. He lifted his eyebrows. "What? You know you're not marrying a stupid man. I'm tracking yours too."

A smile lit Lazarus' face. He shook his head and handed Noir the second box. "Here."

Noir opened it without thinking and only giving it half his attention. He intended to tease Lazarus about not realizing Noir would know his every step. The words froze in his throat as he stared at the open box. A wedding band with deep set diamonds in platinum stared up at him. His chin lifted.

He knew he had to look as shocked as he felt.

Lazarus shifted from one foot to the other. He shoved his hands in his pockets, looking nervous. "I didn't want you to feel cheated out of a Christmas present by me proposing as your gift. Plus, I wasn't really sure you'd even be willing to marry someone like me."

Noir didn't know what to say. There had never been two people more meant to be. They thought so much alike. It was inevitable they would end up here. Noir couldn't find any words, so he walked into Lazarus' arms. "There's no greater gift." He didn't know how to express himself. Noir only hoped Lazarus understood. Lazarus was the biggest blessing he had ever received. His entire life had been showered in riches. He had never felt love before Lazarus gave it to him.

Lazarus squeezed him against his chest and kissed his temple. With his lips pressed to Noir's skin, he spoke softly. "I'll be a good husband. Whatever it takes. You know I'm too obsessive to fail."

A watery chuckle escaped Noir as unexpected tears welled in his eyes. Boredom and unhappiness had driven him for so many years. Sometimes, he didn't know how to handle the feelings Lazarus created inside him. Lazarus would be an amazing husband. Noir knew him. Lazarus genuinely didn't know how to fail. They would never be apart.

Chapter Ten

CARDS MOVED IN LAZARUS' direction. He checked the numbers before eyeing the faces surrounding him. Noir played the part of a bored elitist, eyeing his cards with little concern. It meant nothing to him to lose money in a casino. Lazarus' gaze dropped to the wedding band on Noir's left hand. He smirked. Noir had been his husband for less than two months, but the pride never dimmed. Noir was his greatest possession. Lazarus tore his eyes away from his sexy husband and focused on Heath. Heath was a recent addition to his life. He hadn't cared to meet the guy, but Noir had insisted. Noir had been right. Lazarus genuinely liked the guy. He was caustic and funny. It helped that meeting him had cleared up any doubts in Lazarus' mind. Heath wasn't interested in Noir beyond friendship. Heath didn't seem interested in anything. That was why Lazarus couldn't look away.

Heath glared at a youngish guy at a nearby table. The blond was all flirtatious smiles and touchy hands. He hung on the arm of a man twice his age. Lazarus' first thought was a gold digger, but the man didn't look poor. He fit the crowd.

"Does he owe you money or did he fuck your dog?" Lazarus heard Noir snort at the question. A smile stretched Lazarus' lips. They shared a glance, savoring the memory of their meeting. His gaze returned to Heath.

Heath switched his glare to his cards. "I have no idea what you mean."

Lazarus eyed the man across the room. "Okay, then. Who is he, anyhow?"

"No clue." Heath sounded bored, but his expression said otherwise.

Lazarus looked Noir's way with raised eyebrows.

Noir flashed a sweet smile. Lazarus melted inside. He knew no one else saw this side of Noir. Lazarus almost forgot their topic until Noir answered. "Court Langley. He's a well-known escort. Men get into bidding wars to have him."

Lazarus studied Court. He was beautiful, but so were a lot of people. "Why?"

Heath snorted, proving he harbored more hatred than he wanted them to know.

Noir tapped the table, asking for more cards before responding. "A few reasons, I suppose. He comes from good stock and he's—supposedly—quite well trained in sexual relations."

Lazarus felt the way his eyebrows tried to crawl into his hairline. "What's that supposed to mean?"

"He's a talented whore," Heath said, sounding dry.

"I figured out that much for myself. I meant the good stock thing."

Noir made a dismissive motion. "His father is *the* dentist to the stars. All those pearly white veneers come from somewhere. Everyone goes to him. Therefore, Court is considered one of us."

Lazarus fought an eye roll. Since meeting Noir, Lazarus had been introduced to some of the vainest people he had ever seen.

Everyone competed to be the most beautiful. Meanwhile, all they accomplished was to look exactly alike. The "one of us" comment also sounded a little too cultlike for Lazarus' comfort.

Noir chuckled. "I swear I can hear your thoughts. Not everyone naturally has your sexy body or the confidence to be unique like you." His gaze swept down Lazarus' body. "Not just anyone can pull off those tattoos."

The heat in Noir's stare had Lazarus dropping from the game.

Noir immediately did the same.

Heath groaned. "Newlyweds are so tiresome."

Lazarus barely heard the words. He was already on his feet. Noir was on his heels. They didn't speak or look each other's way. Lazarus veered into the first single stall restroom. Noir didn't hesitate to join him and lock the door behind him. Lazarus fell on him the second they were alone. As his mouth covered Noir's, his hand went straight for the prize. He massaged Noir's cock through his jeans. Lazarus had no qualms about hitting his knees in a public bathroom.

A sexy, needy sound filled the air as Lazarus kissed his way down Noir's body while setting his erection free. Fuck. He never tired of this. From that first night of fucking Noir against the door, Lazarus had been addicted. Any place. Any time. There was no such thing as too much of Noir.

He licked Noir's dick from root to tip before swallowing him. He wasn't sweet or slow. Lazarus devoured Noir. He licked and sucked. Lazarus worshipped. Noir fought the noises leaving him, visibly trying to be quiet. Lazarus didn't want that. He needed

Noir to tell the world no one could please him the way Lazarus did.

Noir cupped the back of Lazarus' head and rode his tongue. "Fuck, Lazarus. That's so good." He babbled something in his native tongue. Lazarus still didn't speak Servenian. He understood certain phrases, though. Noir begged for more. Lazarus wouldn't let him down. For the rest of their lives, Lazarus would always give him more. Nothing else mattered anymore.

Noir never understood what happened between them. It was always this way. One second, they would be doing the most innocuous thing. The next, his dick would be in Lazarus' mouth. No one knew how Noir had begged the universe for him. No way could he have seen Lazarus as the man who would steal his soul. He was so much better than anything Noir could dream.

His mind blanked as his balls drew up tight. Noir couldn't do anything but moan as Lazarus took him to the stars. A loud gasp tore from him as an orgasm stole his ability to make a single sound. All he could do was feel. So much love and elation poured through him. Pleasure rocked his soul. His body practically vibrated with ecstasy. He still shook when Lazarus' mouth covered his again. The taste of his cum waited for him. Noir searched for every drop.

"Goddamn. I love you. That was so fucking hot."

Those should have been Noir's words, but his brain still didn't work properly. "Same." It was all he could croak out. Noir reached for the button on Lazarus' jeans.

Lazarus covered his hand. "This was about you. I'll take mine when we get home."

Noir lost his breath at the promise in Lazarus' tone. He already knew the rest of the day would be him getting fucked.

"I can't tell you how much I love you." Noir bit Lazarus' bottom lip. He knew Lazarus was hungry for him, despite wanting to wait. His post-orgasm happiness had him in a teasing mood. He moved to Lazarus' neck. "I could blow you now and still take it when we get home. Don't you like me on my knees?"

Lazarus smacked his ass. "You're asking for it at this point."

Noir smiled against Lazarus' throat. Before meeting Lazarus, his life had been rage and blood. Since falling in love, all that insanity was pointed straight at Lazarus. There was no level of crazy he wouldn't hit for this man. "You're right." He swiped his hand down the bulge in Lazarus' jeans. "I want it. In my mouth. In my ass while I scream your name. Give me what I want."

"Brat." The grumbled word was all the warning Noir got before he found himself over Lazarus' shoulder again. Lazarus enjoyed this show of alpha possessiveness a bit too much. Noir secretly loved it. No one could see them and not know how they lived for each other. How they belonged to each other.

Lazarus carried him through the casino, uncaring of the looks they received. Their team surrounded them on their way to the door. Noir swore he felt Ajax's eye roll and heard his smile. No matter how much his longtime guard grumbled, Noir knew how Ajax truly felt. He loved Noir, so he loved Lazarus. Without shame, Noir squeezed Lazarus' ass on the way to the door. If he had to suffer getting the wind stolen from him, then Lazarus could handle a little butt fondling.

Lazarus slapped his ass. He didn't hold back. The sound cut through the air. Noir heard someone gasp. He hid a smile against Lazarus' back. He prayed these times between them never ended. The drug dealer and the assassin. They shouldn't work. Life should have destroyed them long ago. Together, they were unstoppable. The greatest love Atlantic City had ever seen.

Keep an eye out for the next Atlantic City's Most Wanted, *Enslaved*.

About the Author

CHARITY PARKERSON IS AN award-winning and multi-published author with several companies. Born with no filter from her brain to her mouth, she decided to take this odd quirk and insert it in her characters. One of her greatest loves is writing morally gray characters. You'll find them scattered throughout her hundreds of titles.

*Eight-time Readers' Favorite Award Winner

*2015 Passionate Plume Award Finalist

*2013 Reviewers' Choice Award Winner

*2012 ARRA Finalist for Favorite Paranormal Romance

*Five-time winner of The Mistress of the Darkpath

Connect with her online:

*Sign up for her newsletter: https://bit.ly/charityparkersonnewsletter

*Join her readers' group on Facebook: http://bit.ly/CharitysTribe

*Website: https://www.charityparkerson.com

*A list of her social media accounts and give-aways all in one place: http://hy.page/charityparkerson